A BIRTHDAY FOR FRANCES

by RUSSELL HOBAN

Pictures by LILLIAN HOBAN

SCHOLASTIC INC.

New York Toronto London Auckland Sydney

ISBN 0-590-06194-1

22 21 20 19 18 17 16 15 14 13   6 7 8 9/8 0/9

Printed in the U.S.A.   09

for Lynn Klotz
who would certainly give
her little sister a Chompo Bar
if she had a little sister

It was the day before
Frances's little sister Gloria's birthday.

Mother and Gloria were sitting at the kitchen table,
making place cards for the party.

Frances was in the broom closet, singing:

Happy Thursday to you,
Happy Thursday to you,
Happy Thursday, dear Alice,
Happy Thursday to you.

"Who is Alice?" asked Mother.

"Alice is somebody that nobody can see,"
said Frances. "And that is why
she does not have a birthday. So I am singing
Happy Thursday to her."

"Today is Friday," said Mother.

"It is Thursday for Alice," said Frances.
"Alice will not have h-r-n-d,
and she will not have g-k-l-s.
But we are singing together."

"What are h-r-n-d and g-k-l-s?" asked Mother.

"Cake and candy. I thought you could spell,"
said Frances.

"I am sure that Alice will have
cake and candy on her birthday," said Mother.

"But Alice does not have a birthday,"
said Frances.

"Yes, she does," said Mother.
"Even if nobody can see her,
Alice has one birthday every year, and so do you.
Your birthday is two months from now.
Then you will be the birthday girl.
But tomorrow is Gloria's birthday,
and she will be the birthday girl."

"That is how it is, Alice," said Frances.
"Your birthday is always the one that is not now."

"Frances," said Mother, "wouldn't you and Alice
like to come out of the broom closet
and help us make place cards for the party?"

Frances came to the table
and sat down and picked up a crayon.

"What are you putting on the place cards?"
she asked.

"Pretty flowers," said Gloria.
"Rainbows and happy trees."

Frances began to draw on a place card,
and as she drew she sang:

   A rainbow and a happy tree
   Are not for Alice or for me.
   I will draw three-legged cats.
   And caterpillars with ugly hats.

Frances stopped singing. "I'm telling," she said.

"Telling what?" said Mother.

"Gloria kicked me under the table,"
said Frances.

"Mean Frances," said Gloria.

"Gloria is mean," said Frances.
"She hid my sand pail and my shovel,
and I never got them back."

"That was last year," said Mother.

"When Gloria is mean, it was always last year,"
said Frances. "But me and Alice know s-m-f-o."

"What is s-m-f-o?" asked Mother.

"Better," said Frances. "Good-bye.
I will be out of town visiting Alice for two weeks,
and I will be back for dinner."

She went to the broom closet
and took out her favorite broom.

"Let's go, Champ," she said. "I'm ready to ride."

Frances climbed onto the broom
and galloped out of the kitchen
while Mother and Gloria finished the place cards.
Then Gloria went out to play
while Mother wrapped her presents in the living room.

Frances was riding back and forth
on her broom on the porch, and as she rode
she sang a song for Alice:

> Everybody makes a fuss
> For birthday girls who are not us.
> Girls who take your pail away
> Eat cake and q-p-m all day.

"Is q-p-m ice cream?" Mother asked Frances
through the window.

"Yes," said Frances. She climbed up
on one of the porch rocking chairs
and looked through the window
at the boxes Mother was wrapping.

"What is Gloria getting from you and from Father
for her birthday?" asked Frances.

"A paintbox and a tea set and a plush pig,"
said Mother.

"I am not going to give Gloria any present,"
said Frances.

"That is all right," said Mother,
and Frances began to cry.

"What is the matter?" said Mother.
"Why are you crying?"

"Everybody is giving Gloria a present but me,"
said Frances.

"Would you like to give Gloria a present?"
said Mother.

"Yes," said Frances. "If I had
my next two allowances, I would have
a nickel and two pennies and another
nickel and two pennies, and I could buy
a Chompo Bar and four balls of bubble gum for Gloria."

"I think it is very nice of you
to want to give Gloria a birthday present,"
said Mother, and she gave Frances
her next two allowances.

That evening Father took Frances
to the candy store to buy a Chompo Bar
and four balls of bubble gum for Gloria.

As they walked home Frances said to Father,
"Are you sure that it is all right
for Gloria to have a whole Chompo Bar?
Maybe she is too young for that kind of candy.
Maybe it will make her sick."

"Well," said Father, "I do not think
it would be good for Gloria to eat Chompo Bars
every day. But tomorrow is her birthday,
and I think it will be
all right for her to eat one."

Frances thought about Gloria and the Chompo Bar,
and while she thought she put
two of the bubble-gum balls into her mouth
without noticing it.
She chewed the bubble gum
and squeezed the Chompo Bar a little.

"Chompo Bars have a soft nougat part inside,"
said Frances, "and there is a chewy caramel part
around that, and the outside is chocolate with nuts.
Probably Gloria could not eat more than half of one."

"Gloria loves sweets," said Father,
"and I am sure that she can eat the whole Chompo Bar.
That is why it is such a good present for her,
and you were very nice to think of it."

"Yes," said Frances,
"and I spent two allowances on Gloria."

While Frances was thinking about the two allowances
she put the other two balls of bubble gum
into her mouth and chewed them,
and she squeezed the Chompo Bar and sang:

> Chompo Bars are nice to get.
> Chompo Bars taste better yet
> When they're someone else's.

"You would not eat Gloria's Chompo Bar,
would you?" said Father.

"It is not Gloria's yet," said Frances.

"I can hardly understand what you are saying,"
said Father. "Is there something in your mouth?"

"I think maybe there is bubble gum,"
said Frances, "but I don't remember
how it got there."

"Maybe I should take care of the Chompo Bar
until you are ready to give it to Gloria,"
said Father.

"All right," said Frances,
and she gave the Chompo Bar to Father
to take care of.

18

The next day was Gloria's birthday,
and the party was that afternoon.
The cake was ready; the table was all set;
and Mother was making hot chocolate.
There were little baskets of gum drops
and chocolate-covered peanuts for everybody.
There were place cards and party poppers
for Mother and Father, for Frances and Gloria,
for Gloria's friend Ida,
and for Frances's friend Albert.

Albert was the first friend to arrive,
and he and Frances sat down in the living room
while they were waiting for Ida.

"What are you giving Gloria?"
Frances asked Albert.

"A little tiny truck in a little tiny box,"
said Albert.

"The kind that costs fifty cents?" asked Frances.

"That's right," said Albert.
"But my mother gave me the money for it."

"I am thinking of giving Gloria a Chompo Bar,"
said Frances. "But I am not sure.
I might and I might not. I had to spend
almost two whole allowances on it."

"That's how it is when it's your own sister,"
said Albert. "I had to spend
my allowance money on my little sister
when she had a birthday.
I gave her a yo-yo. But she is not
high enough off the ground for a yo-yo.
So I get to use it."

"Little sisters are not much r-v-s-m,"
said Frances.

"Good?" said Albert.

"That's right," said Frances.

"No, they are not," said Albert.
"They can't catch. They can't throw.
When you play hide-and-seek, they always hide
in places where part of them is sticking out."

"They take your sand pail and your shovel too,"
said Frances. "They pull the button eyes
off dolls that have button eyes.
They break your crayons so there are no long ones
left in the box. They put water in your mud pies
when you don't want them to.
I don't think many of them deserve a Chompo Bar."

"You can't use a Chompo Bar over and over
like a yo-yo," said Albert. "One time and it's gone.
You should at least get part of it."

"That's right," said Frances.

"Here is Ida now," said Mother,
"and the party can begin."

"When are the presents?" said Gloria
as they all sat down at the places
where their place cards were.

"First," said Father, "your mother
will bring out the cake, and I will light the candles.
Then we will all sing 'Happy Birthday to You.'
Then you make a wish and blow out all the candles.
Then you get your presents."

"I know what to wish," said Gloria.

"Don't tell it," said Ida.

"It won't come true if you do," said Albert.

"Here comes the cake," said Mother.
She put it on the table,
and Father lit the candles.
Then everybody sang "Happy Birthday to You."

Frances did not sing the words
that the others were singing.
Very softly, so that nobody could hear her,
she sang:

Happy Chompo to me
Is how it ought to be —
Happy Chompo to Frances,
Happy Chompo to me.

"Now," said Mother to Gloria, "make your wish
and blow out the candles."

"I want to tell my wish," said Gloria.

"No, no!" said Mother and Father
and Frances and Albert and Ida.

"Just say it inside your head
and blow out the candles," said Albert.

Gloria said her wish inside her head
and blew out all the candles at once.

"Hooray!" said everybody.

"Now your wish will come true," said Mother.

"This is what I wished," said Gloria.
"I wished that Frances would be nice
and not be mad at me because I hid her sand pail
and shovel last year. And I am sorry,
and I will be nice."

"She told," said Ida. "Now her wish won't come true."

"I think it will come true," said Mother,
"because it is a special kind of good wish
that can make itself come true."

"Well," said Frances to Gloria,
"I think your wish will come true too.
And I have a present for you,
and I owe you four balls of bubble gum."

"Now is it time for the presents?" said Gloria.

"Yes," said Father.

Father and Mother gave Gloria the paintbox
and the tea set and the plush pig.
Albert gave her the little tiny truck.
Ida gave her a little china baby doll.
Frances had wrapped the Chompo Bar
in pretty paper and tied it with a ribbon,
and now she got ready to give it to Gloria.

"What is it?" asked Gloria.

"It is something good to eat," said Frances,
"and I will give it to you in a minute.
But first I will sing 'Happy Birthday to You,'
because I did not really sing it before.
Happy birthday to you," sang Frances,
and she squeezed the Chompo Bar.
"Happy birthday to you." Then she stopped
and rested a little.

"You can have a bite when I get it," said Gloria.

Frances took a deep breath and finished the song.
"Happy birthday, dear Gloria, happy birthday to you.
Here," said Frances. She squeezed the Chompo Bar
one last time and gave it to Gloria.

"You can eat it all, because
you are the birthday girl," said Frances.

"Thank you," said Gloria
as she quickly unwrapped the Chompo Bar.
"This is a good present." And she ate it all,
because she was the birthday girl.